go girl

The Big Split

hardie grant EGMONT

The Big Split
first published in 2006
this edition published in 2013 by
Hardie Grant Egmont
Ground Floor, Building 1, 658 Church Street
Richmond, Victoria 3121, Australia
www.hardiegrantegmont.com.au

A CiP record for this title is available from the National Library of Australia

Text copyright © 2006 Rowan McAuley
Illustration and design copyright © 2013 Hardie Grant Egmont

Illustration by Aki Fukuoka
Design by Michelle Mackintosh
Text design and typesetting by Ektavo

Printed in Australia by Griffin Press, an Accredited ISO AS/NZS
14001:2004 Environmental Management System printer.

1 3 5 7 9 10 8 6 4 2

The paper this book is printed on is certified against the
Forest Stewardship Council® Standards. Griffin Press holds
FSC chain of custody certification SGS-COC-005088. FSC
promotes environmentally responsible, socially beneficial
and economically viable management of the world's forests

FSC
www.fsc.org
MIX
Paper from
responsible sources
FSC® C009448

Holly hadn't had her dinner yet, but she felt too weird to eat.

She was bursting with questions, but didn't want to talk to her parents yet.

Holly thought about all the kids she knew whose parents had split up. What did they do, the first night they found out?

Should I call someone?

Billy's mum and dad split up before he was even in kindergarten, so Holly didn't suppose he thought all that much about it now. Olivia's dad had never lived with them in the first place, so that didn't really count. Then she remembered Cassie from tennis camp — her dad moved out just last year.

Holly wondered if she should call Cassie and find out what was supposed to happen next. It would be good to be prepared so her mum and dad couldn't surprise her again like tonight ...

She went to get her diary to dial Cassie's number, but then saw the clock beside her bed. It was far too late to call anyone now. Not even her best friend Lily would be allowed to get a phone call at this time on a school night.

Maybe it's just as well, she thought. *I haven't spoken to Cassie in ages, and I wouldn't know what to say to Lily.*

But of course, there was one person Holly could talk to. Someone who would know exactly how Holly was feeling, and who wouldn't ask lots of hard questions Holly couldn't answer.

She carefully opened her door and peered down the corridor. Good – the house was still quiet.

It was time to go and visit her big sister.

Faith would know what to do.

Chapter Two

Holly wanted to talk to Faith, but for some reason she didn't want her mum or dad to know. She wanted to be private.

Being as sneaky and quiet as she could, she quickly tiptoed to Faith's room and tapped on the door.

'Faith,' she whispered. 'It's me.'

Without waiting for a reply, she opened

the door and slipped inside. She expected Faith to be lying in bed, trying to sleep or sitting around biting her nails just like Holly had been.

To her surprise, though, Faith was doing neither of those things. Faith was packing a suitcase.

'Faith! What are you doing?'

'I'm going with Dad,' said Faith, pulling her underwear drawer right out of the wardrobe and tipping it into her bag.

She dropped the empty drawer beside her bed, and went to pull out the next drawer. This one was all T-shirts and shorts. She dumped it on top of the undies and socks already piled in her bag.

'You're going with Dad?' Holly repeated, stunned. 'How come? And why did he ask you? What about me? Nobody asked me.'

'Nobody asked me, either,' said Faith. 'I decided by myself.'

'And Dad said yes? And Mum agreed?'

'I haven't asked *them*,' said Faith, now heaping her jeans and skirts into the bag. 'I'm just going. Dad can't say no, can he?'

Holly said nothing. She didn't want Faith to leave.

'You could come too, I suppose,' said Faith.

Holly thought about it, then shook her head. 'No. It wouldn't be fair on Mum. She'd be all alone, and that's not right.'

'Right?' snorted Faith. 'Fair? As if any of this is fair!'

They both jumped as someone knocked on the door.

'Girls?'

The door opened. It was their dad,

looking tired and sad. He had his suitcase beside him and the car keys in his hand.

'It's time for me to say goodnight, and well – Faith! What's this?'

'I'm coming too,' said Faith, trying to force the lid of her suitcase down over her mound of clothing.

'Oh, Faith,' said her dad. 'I can't take you with me now, but I promise –'

'Forget it,' said Faith, turning away. She started pulling clothes out of her bag and throwing them angrily across the room.

'But, darling –'

'Forget it, I said! Just go! Don't worry about us. We'll be fine, won't we, Holly?'

Holly looked at them both.

Poor Dad.

Her dad looked sad — sadder than she had ever seen him. Faith looked sad too, but mostly she looked furious. She had her arms crossed and her back to their dad, and her face was bright red.

'Holly?' said her dad.

He reached his hands out to her, and she gave him the biggest hug she could.

There were lots of things she wanted to say, but she didn't know how. She hoped her dad would understand all the things she was feeling from the way she hugged him.

'There's my good girl,' he said, just like he had when she was much younger. He kissed her on the top of her head.

'Faith?'

Faith gave in. Mad as she was, she couldn't ignore him. They hugged and kissed, but then, all too soon, their dad said, 'I have to go now, but I'll call you tomorrow and we'll make plans for the weekend. Be good to your mum.'

And then he was gone.

Chapter Three

The next morning, as Holly got dressed for school, Faith slid into her room. She was still in her pyjamas and had a certain look in her eye that Holly knew well.

'Hey, Holly,' she said in a hushed voice. 'Don't you think we should get a day off?'

'Off what?' asked Holly.

'School, silly. Don't you think we deserve a holiday?'

A holiday sounded good to Holly. 'Have you asked Mum?'

'What? No, of course not. I asked her if she was going to work, and she said yes, so that means she thinks we should go to school too, right? You know what she's like.'

It was true. Their mum was always going on about how important school was. She *always* made them go to school, even the time Holly got so sunburnt she could hardly sit down.

'Well, if we don't ask, then what?' asked Holly.

'We wag.'

'What!'

'Holly! Faith! Are you two ready for breakfast?' their mum called out from the kitchen.

'Nearly!' Faith called back, cheerfully. Then she hissed to Holly, 'We'll talk later. Just make sure you eat heaps of brekkie.'

Holly had never wagged school in her life. She had to admit, though, she really didn't want to go to school.

She had lain in bed last night, trying to imagine what she would say to her best friend, Lily. How could she explain that her parents had suddenly split up?

Lily's mum and dad were still together.

Whenever Holly went to play at Lily's on the weekends, she saw them laughing and joking around together. It was as if they were best friends, like Holly and Lily, and not just parents.

Holly thought they were perfect, like a family on TV.

No, she decided. Lily wouldn't understand. And if Lily didn't understand, then why would anyone else?

That made Holly's mind up.

She sneaked up to Faith, who was finally getting dressed, and whispered, 'OK, I'll do it – let's wag!'

Holly's mum was a vet, and her clinic was in the middle of the shops that ran along the main road. Each morning, she drove to work, and Holly and Faith got out at the bakery and then walked an extra block to the bus stop.

That morning, Faith stopped outside the bakery, and waited until their mum drove on. Then she said to Holly, 'OK, I've worked it out. The first thing is, how much money do you have? I've only got about $3.00.'

Holly felt in her bag for her wallet.

'I've got $6.50.'

'That's heaps! Right, so here's what we should do. We go into the bakery and buy ourselves some extra lunch. After that, we just do whatever we like until school finishes and then we meet Mum back at the clinic.'

'But what will we do?' asked Holly.

'I don't know. We'll have to go where no-one can see us, though. Otherwise they might tell the school or phone Mum.'

How do you wag school?

'Hey, we could sneak down the back of the park and go for a bush walk,' said Holly.

'Yes! That's perfect. We could go to that big rock by the water and hang out there until it's home time.'

Holly couldn't quite believe they were really going to go through with it. She was actually starting to feel a bit excited.

Could they really skip a whole day of school? It would be by far the naughtiest thing they had ever done …

'Come on,' said Faith, walking into the bakery. 'I want a lamington for lunch. Maybe two!'

Holly followed her sister.

Chapter Four

In the bakery, Holly stood nervously near the door. Other people were already lined up to be served, and she didn't want any of them to notice her. She pulled the hood of her jacket up over her head.

A business woman ordered a birthday cake, a postman bought a sausage roll, and the lady from the paper shop was waiting for some bread.

Holly fidgeted. What if one of the parents from school came in and saw them? Or worse, one of the teachers? Or worst of all, what if their mum dropped by to buy her lunch before she started work?

Maybe this wasn't such a good idea.

I hope no-one sees me.

It didn't matter how awful it would be at school, having to explain about her mum and dad. It *had* to be better than this sick, guilty feeling growing in Holly's tummy.

Faith didn't seem to think so, though. She just looked happy and excited.

'Look!' she said to Holly. 'We have enough money for a cheese-and-bacon roll each, and a lamington, and we'll still have enough money left over for icy poles later.'

'Faith, maybe we should –'

'No way,' said Faith, before she could finish. 'I don't care what you're about to say. I'm going. You can catch the bus to school if you want, but I've made up my mind.'

What could Holly do?

It was hard to argue with Faith. And if Holly went to school by herself, someone might ask her where Faith was, and then what would she say?

'OK,' she said hesitantly. 'Let's go.'

'Excellent,' said Faith.

They tucked their lunch into their school bags and started walking to the park. Holly kept looking over her shoulder.

'Act natural!' hissed Faith. 'No-one will even notice us, as long as you stop looking so guilty and suspicious!'

Holly tried. But every step of the way, she expected someone to grab her by the shoulder and say, 'Now then, young lady. What are you up to?'

But no-one did.

They walked through the park and down to the beginning of the path into the bush. Holly had one last quick look to

see if anyone was watching, and then they were in among the trees.

'We made it!' she said.

'I told you so,' said Faith. 'But come on – I want to get to the big rock.'

They clomped along the path. It was weird to be doing a bushwalk in their school shoes and carrying their school bags. Normally they did this walk on weekends with their dad. Holly didn't want to think about that right now.

The big rock seemed extra quiet and lonely today. On weekends, they often saw other people bushwalking or paddling a canoe along the river.

Today, the bush felt completely empty.

It was just Holly and Faith, the trees and a couple of buzzing flies.

'Brilliant!' said Faith, sitting down and taking her shoes and socks off.

She wriggled her bare toes in the sun.

Holly heard a noise behind her and spun around to see who was there. It was only a lizard rustling through the leaves.

'Relax,' said Faith. 'No-one's going to find us.'

'All right,' said Holly, sitting down too. 'I suppose I could do my maths home-work. I didn't get a chance last night with all the … well, you know.'

Faith snorted. 'You're hopeless – you don't even know how to wag properly.

You're not meant to do your homework!'

But Holly ignored her. It was good to have something to do. Otherwise she might start thinking about her mum and dad.

Chapter Five

Spending the whole day in the bush alone with Faith was harder than Holly had imagined. For a start, they had to stay hidden, so when they realised they didn't have any water with them, there was nothing to do but be thirsty. And Holly needed to go to the toilet.

'I could sneak back to the park and find a tap,' said Holly. 'I know there's a toilet near the swings.'

'No,' said Faith. 'We can't risk getting caught now. We'll just have to wait until school's out.'

But neither of them had a watch, and it was hard to tell how much longer they had to go. It felt like hours since they had eaten their cheese-and-bacon rolls and lamingtons – plus the ordinary lunch their mum had packed them that morning – and Holly's stomach was rumbling loudly.

'Can't you be quiet?' grouched Faith.

'I can't help it!'

'Urgh, this is boring.'

Once Holly had finished her home-work, they had started a competition to see who could throw a stick far enough to land in the river. They had played the game for so long, there wasn't a single stick left on the big rock.

Now that even that game was over, there was *really* nothing to do.

'When do you think we can go back? It must be home time soon.'

'I think we should wait a bit longer,' said Faith. 'It's better to be a bit late than too early.'

'But I'm busting! And starving! And thirsty!'

'Oh, you're such a sook!'

'I am not!'

'Fine. Whatever. Let's go,' said Faith,

starting to put her shoes back on. 'Even if we do get caught, at least I won't have to listen to you whinge any more!'

Holly bit her lip. It was no use talking to Faith when she was cranky. And the truth was, she was getting a bit bored of Faith, too.

They trudged back through the bush to the park. Of course, it was all uphill this way, and the sun was hotter now than it had been that morning. By the time they got to the public toilets, they were thirstier and crankier than ever.

Holly ran the last little bit and locked herself into the toilet cubicle with a sigh of relief. After she had washed her hands at the sink, she and Faith stood for ages at the bubbler, taking turn after turn to drink down the lovely, cool water. Then they started walking back up to the shops.

'Do you think school's out yet?' asked Holly. 'Everything looks a bit quiet.'

'Yeah, I know,' said Faith, being a bit friendlier now that she wasn't so thirsty. 'Maybe we should try to hide out a bit more until –'

'YOU! Faith! Holly!'

Holly stopped dead in the middle of the footpath.

Uh-oh, she thought. She knew exactly who it was shouting, but she really, *really* didn't want to turn around and see.

'I'm talking to you! Don't pretend you can't hear me!'

Reluctantly, Holly turned around.

There, marching towards them with a terrible look on her face, was their mum. She looked furious. In fact, Holly hadn't seen her so mad since that time she and Faith had decided to make their own indoor water slide on the kitchen floor with a whole bottle of strawberry bubble-bath and two litres of milk.

'Erm ... hello, Mum,' said Holly, weakly.

'Hello?' yelled her mum. 'Hello? What sort of thing to say is that? Do you know how worried I've been? The school called this morning to find out where you both were, and I didn't know, because I *thought* you were at school. What happened? Where were you? Where have you been?'

Holly was used to her mum getting cross sometimes, but this was different. This time, her mum looked really upset, too. Holly had been feeling a bit guilty about wagging, but now she saw how worried and sad her mum was, she felt ashamed.

'Sorry, Mum,' she whispered, staring at her feet.

She expected her mum to yell some more, but instead she heard a sniffing noise. She looked up and saw her mum quickly wiping away a tear.

'I was so worried,' she said in a softer voice. 'Everything's been so mixed up and crazy at home, and then I thought I'd lost you two as well ...'

'I'm sorry,' Holly said again. She wished they'd never wagged. It wasn't even that much fun at the time and it certainly wasn't worth it now.

'So where were you?' asked her mum.

I should never have wagged school.

'We went down to the bush,' said Faith. 'We didn't want to go to school. We wanted a day off.'

'Why didn't you say so?' asked their mum. 'We could all have taken a day off together, if only you'd asked.'

'We didn't want to bother you,' said Holly.

'We thought you'd say no,' said Faith.

'Well,' said their mum. 'What's done is done. I'm just glad you're safe,' and she gave them both big, relieved hugs.

'And now,' she went on, 'let's get back to the clinic. I have a funny feeling you two are going to be busy all afternoon, cleaning out the dog kennels and cat boxes.'

'What?!' Faith protested. 'Not that! Oh, Mum!'

But Holly stamped on her foot. 'Shh!' she hissed. 'Do as she says. We're lucky if that's all the trouble we get into.'

And they followed their mum back to the clinic.

Chapter Six

That night, their dad rang. Their mum spoke to him first, and Holly heard her tell him everything. It took a long time. She didn't leave out any of the details.

Eventually, though, she passed the phone to Holly.

'So,' said her dad. 'You've been up to no good with your sister.'

'Yeah,' Holly admitted.

'What were you thinking, Holl? Your poor mother. This is a hard time for her, and you and Faith need to be especially kind.'

'Kind to *her*?' said Holly, suddenly cross. 'Who's being kind to us? We weren't trying to be mean to Mum. We just didn't want to go to school.'

This isn't fair.

Her dad sighed. 'It's hard on you kids, too, I know. Nobody's having a good time right now. But things will get better. I promise, Holly.'

Yeah, right, thought Holly. *But when?*

Holly sat in the hallway and listened while Faith had her turn on the phone. It was easy to guess what their dad was saying from what Faith said in reply.

'As if we got away with anything!' Faith protested. 'First Mum yells at us in front of practically the whole of Australia. *Then* we have to spend nearly two hours shovelling dog poop at the clinic. *And* some of the dogs had diarrhoea! Then Mum tells us she's phoned the school and everyone agrees that Holly and I should be on lunchtime detention for the rest of the week!'

Then Faith went silent.

Holly poked her head into the room just in time to see Faith roll her eyes at something their dad had said. He must have really been telling her off.

'It's fine for you to say that, Dad, but it doesn't make it any better for Holly and me, does it?'

There was another pause as Faith listened, and then she said in a softer voice, 'I know. I miss you, too. Love you. Bye.'

'Well?' said Holly as her sister hung up the phone.

'He agrees we should do the detention. And he wants to take us out to the movies on Friday night.'

'So that's it, then. We have to go to school tomorrow.'

'Yep,' grumbled Faith.

Holly sighed.

The next day, Holly woke up to the sound of an argument.

Is Dad home? she wondered. But it wasn't her dad she heard, it was Faith.

'I do feel sick, Mum. In my stomach.'

'That's enough, Faith. You're going to school.'

And then the sound of Faith grumbling, stomping down the corridor, and slamming her bedroom door.

A moment later, Holly's mum came into her room and sat down on the end of her bed.

'And how about you?' she asked. 'Are you going to try to tell me you're too sick for school as well?'

'No.'

'And no wagging either, right?'

'No!' Holly didn't think she and Faith were ever going to be allowed to forget about yesterday.

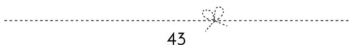

'OK, then. Get up and have brekkie. I don't want you to be late today.'

There was no way of avoiding it any longer. Holly was going to have to go to school. And that meant talking to people. And talking to people meant that she would have to admit to herself that her dad had really left. Her parents really were splitting up.

Holly wasn't looking forward to that one little bit.

Chapter Seven

At school, as usual, Holly and Faith went their separate ways as soon as they got to the playground. Even though Faith was two years older than Holly, the way their birthdays worked out, she was only one year ahead at school. Holly was in Mr Mack's class, and Faith was in Miss Price's.

All the kids agreed – Miss Price was scary. She was quiet and serious, and her lessons were very dull. She didn't laugh or tell jokes, and Faith said she hardly ever smiled.

Holly felt really sorry for her sister being in that class.

Miss Price's class usually hung out by the tennis courts, so Faith went that way. Holly turned and saw her group over by the trees, playing handball.

Phew, she thought. If everyone was busy playing, she could sneak in and join in the game and hopefully not have to say anything at all.

She saw that Lily was in king, about to serve the ball. Then Lily looked up and saw Holly walking over.

Holly expected her to maybe wave hello and keep on playing, but Lily threw the ball to Iris.

'You play king,' Lily said to Iris, who was in queen. 'I need to talk to Holly.'

Lily hurried over to Holly. Holly could hear the other girls calling to Iris, 'Service! Service!' but Lily wasn't taking any notice of them.

'Where were you yesterday?' she said. 'Were you sick? You didn't call me!'

Holly hadn't realised how much her friend would miss her. She had been so worried Lily wouldn't understand about her mum and dad, she had forgotten Lily only really cared about *her*.

Holly thought how dumb she'd been to forget what a great friend Lily was. Of course she could tell her all about her dad leaving – she could tell Lily anything!

'Well, you'll never guess what happened,' Holly began.

And she told Lily everything. About her mum and dad fighting, and then her dad leaving, and then wagging school and

This is what friends are for.

hanging out in the bush, and then getting into trouble with everyone.

Lily didn't say a word. She just listened and listened as Holly spoke, her eyes getting bigger and bigger with amazement.

'Wow,' she said, when Holly had finished. 'Holly, that's a really big deal.'

'I know.'

'No wonder you wagged yesterday. So, do you want to keep it a secret, or are you going to let other people know?'

Holly grinned.

Lily understood perfectly. And because Lily understood, suddenly Holly didn't care who else knew.

She shrugged. 'I suppose, if it comes up …'

'Hey, guys,' said Layla, jogging over to them. 'If what comes up?'

'Oh,' said Lily. 'You heard …'

She looked sideways at Holly to see what she should do. Holly just shrugged again. She didn't mind at all now.

'Well,' said Lily. 'Holly's mum and dad have split up.'

'No way!'

'What? What?' It was Aysha, Layla's twin, walking by and overhearing them.

Layla passed on the news. In this way, one by one, Holly's whole class knew in about five minutes.

This was exactly what Holly had been dreading – everyone talking about her, everyone knowing about her family's private business. She had thought she would hate it, but it turned out to be OK.

Better than OK, actually.

It was good not to have to keep a secret. And it was good to know that nobody thought differently about Holly just because of her parents. No matter what her mum and dad did, she was still just Holly. Nobody could change that.

Chapter Eight

In the car on the way home from school that afternoon, Holly sat in the front seat with her mum.

'How was school?' asked her mum.

'It was OK.'

'Just OK?'

'Well, I would have said it was good, but I had detention at lunch, remember?'

'I remember. How was it?'

Holly sighed. 'Boring. We had to sit in Mrs Delano's classroom and do silent work. And I had heaps to do, because Mr Mack had collected all my worksheets from yesterday.'

'How about you, Faith?' asked her mum, calling over her shoulder to the back seat.

Faith grunted. She was in a bad mood.

'Faith?' said their mum. 'What happened today?'

Faith didn't say anything, but Holly heard a sniff from the back seat. Holly turned around to look and saw that Faith was crying!

'Faith!' said Holly. 'What's wrong? Was Miss Price mean to you?'

Faith shook her head and looked out the window. They drove the last few blocks in silence, and then their mum pulled into the driveway at home. She turned off the engine, took off her seatbelt and turned around so she could see Faith too.

'What's happened, baby?'

Faith got cross then.

'What do you think?' she yelled. 'What do you think I'm upset about?'

'It *was* Miss Price, wasn't it?' said Holly.

'No!' Faith yelled again. 'Nothing to do with school! As if I care about stupid Miss Price!'

'Well, what then, honey?' said their mum in a calm, soothing voice.

'You!' said Faith. 'You and Dad! I don't want you to be split up! Can't you get back together?'

Their mum sighed. 'I'm sorry, Faith, but no. It's very complicated –'

'Why? What's complicated about it? When Holly and I fight, you always say we're sisters and we're stuck with each other. You say we have to work it out and be friends. Why is it different with you and Dad?'

Holly thought that was a very good point. She was curious to know what her mum would say.

'I think we'd better go inside and have a proper talk,' said her mum.

Inside, Holly and Faith sat at the kitchen table while their mum made three glasses of cordial. She brought the whole biscuit tin to the table, too, which was normally out of bounds for afternoon tea.

'Right,' she said, sitting down. 'Let's talk.'

At that very moment, the phone rang.

'Hang on …' she said, getting up again. 'Hello? Oh, it's you. I think you should come over. The girls need to talk to us. OK. See you soon.'

She hung up the phone and looked back at Holly and Faith.

'That was your dad. He'll be here in about twenty minutes, and then we can all talk together. Go and get started on your homework. We'll get takeaway for dinner.'

'Wow, Faith,' whispered Holly as they went to their rooms. 'How did you make that happen?'

'I don't know, but let's be on our best behaviour. Maybe if we're good, we can get Dad to stay.'

Chapter Nine

Their dad rang the doorbell when he arrived, instead of letting himself in with his key as he usually would. Holly thought that was a bad sign. Still, she and Faith ran to him and pulled him inside.

'Mum said we could have Thai for dinner,' said Faith. 'You have to help us choose!'

Holly could see her dad felt awkward. He looked like he wasn't sure what to do or where to sit.

That's crazy! thought Holly. *This is his home, too!*

But then, it wasn't really. Not anymore. She had to try to remember that.

She wanted to be like Faith – confident that their dad might change his mind and stay with them. But she couldn't ignore how uncomfortable her mum and dad looked with each other.

'Well,' said her mum, as though it was a big effort to sound cheerful. 'Why don't you three organise dinner? Then we can talk while we wait for it to get here.'

Faith and her dad argued over the menu.

'I want Pad Thai and Mee Grob,' said Faith.

'But those are both noodle dishes,' said her dad. 'We can't have two lots of noodles.'

'Why not? Noodles are my favourite!'

'You choose one, and we'll let Holly pick something. Holly?'

But Holly didn't want to choose. She was too busy watching and listening, trying to figure out how her family fit together. Were they still a family if they didn't live together?

Her dad saw the sad look on her face and said, 'All right, let's hurry up and get dinner. Then we can have this talk.'

Once he had made the phone call to order dinner, they all sat down at the table.

'So, where should we start?' asked her mum.

'How about,' said Faith, 'you explain to Holly and me why you and Dad can't just stay together?'

Holly saw her mum and dad look at each other.

'It's complicated –' her dad started, but Faith cut in.

'That's exactly what Mum said! But why? What is so tricky about being nice to each other?'

Their mum sighed. She was sighing a lot lately, now that Holly thought about it.

'Dad and I have tried,' she said. 'Really, we have. We wish we could make it work, too, but things have been cross and unhappy for so long now.'

Their dad nodded and went on. 'Do you remember all those nights you had dinner at Auntie Pia's? Mum and I were trying to sort stuff out with a counsellor, trying to make things better. But in the end, we decided we needed some time apart.'

Something was puzzling Holly and at last she realised what it was.

'But you're getting on now!' she said. 'You don't look cross with each other right now. And I've heard you talking on the phone, and you don't argue at all anymore.

Maybe it did work. Maybe it will all be OK after all!'

Her dad smiled sadly. 'That's our point, though, Holly. Mum and I get on better when we're not together. The longer we're together, the more we argue and yell, and we don't want you girls growing up in a house where there's fighting all the time.

'We want you to see that your mum and dad can be friends with each other,' he went on. 'Even if that means we have to live in different houses.'

'Do you understand?' asked their mum.

It was confusing.

Holly thought it sounded like it made sense in her head, but in her heart she just wanted them to stay together.

'I don't know,' Holly said, slowly. 'I sort of know what you mean ...'

'And Faith?' said their mum. 'What do you think?'

Holly turned to face her sister. What would Faith have to say about all this?

Chapter Ten

'You want to know what I think?' said Faith. 'You *really* want to know?'

Her mum and dad nodded. 'Yes, Faith. We want you to tell us how you feel.'

'OK, then,' said Faith. 'I think it's all a bunch of lies!'

'Faith!' gasped her dad.

Holly stared at her sister, amazed. She was shocked that Faith would be so blunt, but she was also glad. It was good to hear Faith saying what Holly really wanted to say.

'Well, I do,' Faith went on. 'I don't care what you and Mum say. I know exactly what's going to happen. I talked about it with the kids at school, and we worked it all out.'

'So what's going to happen?' asked her mum. 'I mean, what do the kids at school *think* is going to happen?'

Faith looked sternly at her parents and folded her arms.

'Right,' she said. 'First of all, you and Dad aren't going to stay friends. You're saying that now to make Holly and me feel better, but it isn't true.

'Second, Dad is going to get a new job. Probably in America. And then we'll never see him again.

'Then, after Dad goes to America, we'll have to sell our home and move to some horrible place where we don't know anyone and go to a new school.'

Faith drew a deep breath, but she hadn't finished yet. 'And after that, you'll get a boyfriend, Mum. And then you'll marry him, and you'll have a new baby, and you'll be your own special family. Except for Holly and me. You'll forget about us.'

Holly felt like she was going to faint.

'Is that true?' she asked. 'Is that really how it's going to be?'

'Yes,' said Faith.

'NO!' said their mum and dad at the same time. 'No! Definitely not!'

'Never!' said their dad. 'Of course your mum and I want to stay friends. We were friends long before we got married. And I'm not changing my job. And even if I did, I wouldn't go to America. I want to stay close by my girls. I don't want to miss out on you two growing up!'

'All right, then,' said Faith, and then looked at her mum.

'Well?' said Faith.

'Well, we're not selling the house, that's for sure,' said her mum. 'Dad and I have discussed it, and we're staying right here.

Money's going to be a bit tight for a while, but we don't want to move house on top of everything else. Nothing's going to change there.'

Phew, thought Holly. She loved her bedroom and the backyard, and she didn't want to change schools, either.

So far, so good.

Maybe it will be OK?

What else would her mum say?

'As for a boyfriend, well, I don't plan to have one. Not for a long time, anyway. And if I ever did want to go out with someone – not that I'm planning to! – I'd be very careful that they were someone you two could like.'

'See?' Faith said to Holly, rolling her eyes. 'I told you. Mum can't promise us there won't be a boyfriend or babies to take our place.'

'No, of course not,' said their dad. 'It would be silly for your mum or me to try to look into the future. We don't want to pretend with you or make things up. We want to tell you the truth, and the truth is, one day, your mum or I might possibly meet someone new —'

'Aha!' said Faith, angrily. 'You admit it!'

'*But*,' said their dad, 'we *can* promise that we will always love you. No-one will ever forget about you or Holly. We won't ever stop loving you or thinking how beautiful and smart and wonderful you both are.'

'Your dad's right,' said their mum. 'It wouldn't matter if there were fifty new babies in our family, you would always be our girls. There will never, ever be another Faith or Holly to take your places.'

Chapter Eleven

Holly realised she was holding her breath. She had been concentrating so hard on what everyone was saying, she had forgotten to breathe. Her mum and dad and Faith looked tense and focused, too.

It was the most scary and interesting conversation Holly had ever been part of. She felt like her mum and dad were really treating Faith and her like grown-ups.

It made her feel sort of strong and brave to know they thought she was old enough for the truth.

She couldn't wait to hear what was going to happen next.

Faith was thinking over what her mum and dad had been saying.

'Well, OK,' she said. 'But I still wish you could tell us now how things are going to work out.'

'So do we, honey,' said their dad. 'But we can't make promises about the future. Mum and I don't know what's around the corner.'

Holly spoke up. 'That means things could change again, doesn't it? Things are changing now, but they could keep on changing, couldn't they?'

'That's right,' said her mum. 'But that's how life always is. Nobody ever knows exactly how it's going to turn out.'

Holly hadn't thought of that before. Up until now, life had seemed to be pretty ordinary. It was part of growing up, she supposed, understanding that nothing would stay the same forever.

Just then, the doorbell rang.

'That'll be dinner!' said her mum. 'I almost forgot.'

'I didn't,' said her dad. 'I'm starving after all this talking!'

Holly jumped up from the table with

her mum, and grabbed the money off the bench as she went. Her mum opened the front door, and there was a teenager, holding up two white plastic bags of hot food.

'Hi, Paul,' said Holly's mum.

They often got food from the same restaurant and it was usually Paul who delivered it. He had a black leather jacket, and long black hair tied back in a ponytail, and he delivered the food on a black-and-silver motorcycle. Holly could hear its engine growling in the driveway.

Paul was so good looking, Holly shivered every time she saw him.

Shyly, and without saying a word, she held the money out to him.

'Thanks, squirt!' he said, taking the money and handing her the food. 'See you next time.'

Holly felt herself go red with embarrassment, but that didn't stop her from watching him walk back to his motorcycle.

'He's gorgeous, isn't he?' said her mum as she shut the door.

'Mum!' squealed Holly. 'Gross! Don't even say it!'

But it reminded her that her mum and dad were right – you could never tell what was going to happen next.

One minute Holly had been in the middle of a very serious and grown-up conversation, thinking so hard about her mum and dad splitting up, it was as if the rest of the world had stopped existing. And the next minute she had forgotten all about that, and was dreaming instead of riding with Paul on the back of his motorbike.

'Come on!' laughed her mum. 'The food will get cold if you stand there much longer!'

'Mum …' groaned Holly, following her back out to the kitchen.

Chapter Twelve

Somehow, after dinner that night, things seemed calmer in Holly's family. She and Faith went and saw their dad's new flat on the weekend. They worked out their bedrooms and how they wanted to decorate them.

Their dad didn't have much furniture yet, so they ended up having a picnic dinner on the living-room floor with take-away pizza.

'Next time you come over, I'll have beds for you both,' he said. 'And I'll cook you a proper meal, and you can stay over, if you want.'

'But don't get any tables or chairs,' said Holly. 'I like sitting on the floor. It's more relaxing.'

'Yeah,' said Faith. 'You could just have beanbags and cushions. As long as you didn't have soup, it would be great.'

'I'll think about it,' smiled their dad. 'But for now, I think I'd better drive you home. I don't want to keep you up too late on our first visit.'

That night in bed, Holly thought about all the changes that were going on. She had been a bit scared at first, but now she could see that not every change was bad. For example, now she was going to have *two* bedrooms – that would be cool. And it had been nice, too, to have her dad all to herself and Faith.

She began to feel better about the idea that things were changing all the time.

As if to prove the point, that Tuesday, coming back from school with Faith, another change was waiting at the clinic.

Beside their mum's desk was a big cardboard box, full of scuffling, yapping noises. Someone must have dropped off another litter of puppies. Holly and Faith ran to have a look.

'Oh, how sweet!' said Faith. 'Can we have one?'

Holly sighed. Whenever a litter of puppies or kittens was left at the clinic, Faith *always* asked for one. And their mum *always* said no. Faith never gave up, but Holly was so used to the routine that she had stopped listening.

This time, though, she heard Faith gasp. 'What did you say?'

Their mum smiled broadly. 'I said yes. Now it's just us girls at home, we don't have to worry about your dad's hay fever anymore.'

'I don't believe it!' said Faith. 'You mean we can really have a puppy?'

'Better than that,' said their mum. 'These are only going to be little dogs. You can choose one each.'

'Two dogs!' cheered Holly.

I'm going to choose you!

'Yes,' said their mum. 'That way they can keep each other company when you're at school all day.'

Holly thought that was an excellent idea because, even for dogs, there was nothing quite like having a sister to stick with you when things got tough and lonely.

With all the excitement of decorating their new rooms and having new puppies to play with, it took a while for life to settle down.

Holly felt as though the days had been racing by, and there seemed to be so many new things to think about and do – helping her dad pick out a sofa and curtains, going to puppy training, learning how to use a paint roller, helping her mum out more with the cooking ...

Holly really couldn't say that *anything* had got back to normal since her parents had split up. But slowly, she realised that they had invented a new kind of normal. And not only was Holly getting used to it, she even *liked* it.

She noticed that her mum had stopped sighing so much, and started singing around the house instead. And although she sometimes missed her dad during the week, she got in the habit of calling him

after school, and they ended up talking more on the phone than they ever had when he was living at home.

Most importantly, there were no more arguments at home, and Holly's mum and dad were able to talk to one another in a new way.

It was just what they had hoped for.

One evening, playing with their puppies, Holly and Faith talked it over.

'I thought it would wreck everything if Mum and Dad split up,' said Holly. 'But we're OK, aren't we?'

'Of course we are,' said Faith, letting her puppy lick her face.

'I was worried for a while that we wouldn't be a real family if we didn't all live together, but I think I was wrong.'

'Well, duh!' said Faith. 'I mean, Auntie Pia and Uncle David don't live with us, but they're still our family.'

'Hey, I didn't think of that!'

'And Dad promised, didn't he, that he'd always be our dad, no matter what.'

'Yeah, that's right,' said Holly happily, stroking her own puppy. 'We're still a proper family. We're just a bit more spread out than we used to be.'

Collect them all!

Sleep-over

Boy friend?

Surf's Up

Sister Spirit

Dancing Queen

Flower Girl

Camp Chaos

Best Christmas Ever

Back to School

The Worst Gymnast

Sink or Swim

Music Mad

Class Captain

The New Girl

Karate Kicks

Secret's Out

www.gogirlhq.com